Maisie and the Monster

12·4·90. Best wishes to Kirsten from
Aileen Paterson and maisie × ×

One summer day, the 23 bus was making its way towards Morningside. Maisie Mackenzie, her Granny and their neighbour, Mrs McKitty, sat at the front on the top deck. Maisie always pretended to be the driver when they got that seat. They had enjoyed a busy day shopping. Maisie had joined the Morningside Brownies and was going away next day on her pack holiday. She like the Brownies and she liked her uniform and her little woolly hat with the bobble on top.

"You'll need some warm vests and new wellies," Granny had said at breakfast.

"And I'll need plenty sweeties," replied Maisie.
Now as they returned, Mrs McKitty extolled the joys of Inverness-shire where the holiday was to be.

"Oh, I do love the Highlands," she crooned. "My husband, Cecil, and I were frequent visitors to Drumnadrochit. The scenery and the Highland hospitality are

so wonderful." She cast a sharp look at Maisie, who was busy turning an imaginary steering-wheel. "I do hope, Maisie, that you will be a credit to Edinburgh."

And so she talked all the way home, pausing only to give the driver a ticking-off about his driving as they got off the bus.

When they got back to the flat, Granny made a pot of tea, while Mrs McKitty fetched in her budgie—he had been left alone all day and missed the company—then Maisie sat down to read a letter which had arrived when they were out. It was from her Daddy, who was exploring in a jungle.

"Dear Maisie," the letter began, "I've been on an expedition to Lake Bamalama, up North. It's the rainy season here and our camp was waterlogged. It got so bad that we abandoned our tents and sheltered in some caves. I discovered that I was sharing my cave with a gigantic snake!"

At this, Granny squealed and threw her pinny over her head. Billy flapped and screeched around his cage, and Mrs McKitty patted her face with her hanky.

"What a pity your Daddy doesn't have a nice clean job in the Morningside Bank," she gasped.

Maisie cleared her throat and continued.

"It was most interesting, and the snake was very tame and friendly."

Granny reappeared from under her pinny and Maisie read the rest of the letter, which was all about the animals and the fierce warrior tribes he had met. The two old lady cats shook their heads and said how glad they were that they lived in Edinburgh. Maisie said nothing, but she secretly hoped that she would have an

adventure when *she* was away.

Next morning, Granny and Mrs McKitty took Maisie down to where the mini-bus was waiting to take the Brownies away on holiday. Brown Owl checked her list, to make sure that everyone was there.

"Right-ho, Maisie. Now we're ready to go. Flora and Effie are here, and Emily and Frances McFluff, Bunty Black, Morag McTavish . . ."

When everybody was aboard the bus, they waved goodbye. Brown Owl tooted the horn and off they went. Soon Morningside was left behind and the Brownies began to sing.

"Ging-gang-goolly, goolly, goolly on a push-bike,
Ging-gang-goo, Ging-gang-goo;
Ging-gang-goolly, goolly, goolly on a push-bike,
Ging-gang-goo, ging-gang-goo;
Pedal, oh pedal faster, oh pedal faster up the hill,
Pedal, oh pedal faster, oh pedal faster up the hill,
Here we go, here we go, here we go, here we go—
Puncture, puncture, puncture, puncture . . ."

By now Edinburgh itself was left behind and they were travelling through open country. As they got to the Forth Road Bridge, another mini-bus came alongside and it was full of Cubs. In it, waving to them, were Archie and Hector, on the way to their Cub Camp.

Maisie and the Brownies waved back and cheered.

"Morningside will be quiet with all of us away," said Effie.

"I bet Mrs McKitty will be pleased," laughed Maisie.

The Brownies' mini-bus picked up speed and pulled away from the Cubs. It headed north and the kittens enjoyed their trip—looking at the view, eating sandwiches and passing round sweeties. Wee Effie got out her story book and Flora read aloud to her and Maisie. The story was all about a fierce dragon. Effie's eyes grew wide as she listened.

"Miaow," she squeaked, "I'm frightened of dragons. They've got terrible habits. They smoke and roar and eat kittens for their tea."

"Huh!" scoffed Maisie, "I could knock the spots off a dragon, any time."

Flora smiled, remembering how Maisie had been full of bravado at Hallowe'en. Until . . .

It was evening by the time they arrived at a forest clearing near Loch Ness. The bus drew up beside a big log cabin and they got out and took their things into the cabin. There were little bunk beds with red blankets and a stove for cooking, a long table and chairs. After they had unpacked, they washed their paws and whiskers, had a simple supper which Brown Owl rustled up, then went to bed as they were all so tired after the journey. But Maisie was so excited, she could hardly sleep. She couldn't wait for the next day, when she would begin exploring.

"This is going to be a great adventure," she thought.

But, when they woke, the rain was pouring down and there was a rumble of thunder from the dark grey sky. It rained non-stop for days. Brown Owl organised games

and they cooked in the little kitchen in the hut and told stories by lamplight. But every day it was too wet and muddy to go outside for walks, or to play, even in their wellies. Maisie grew very bored. She tried to do her knitting for her knitter's badge, but she wasn't very good at it. The wool tangled round her legs, stitches dropped and strange lumpy bits appeared for no reason and had to be ripped down and

begun again. She got very grumpy, especially when it was her turn to clean the kitchen and wash the dishes.

"This isn't much fun," she grumbled to Flora.

"Cheer up, Maisie," said her friend. "It can't rain for ever."

"Would you like another game of snakes and ladders?" asked Effie. Maisie shook her head dejectedly and lay down on her bunk, listening to the rain drumming on the roof.

One morning, she was wakened by Flora, excitedly shaking her.

"Wake up, Maisie, wake up. The sun's out today!"

"Yippee!" shouted Maisie, leaping out of bed and full of beans again. It was indeed a lovely day and the Brownies set out for a walk in the forest. Maisie was full of high spirits and kept dashing into the bracken.

"You must stay with the others," said Brown Owl. "We'll have to stick together and keep to the path today, because the undergrowth is still very wet and muddy."

But Maisie didn't think very much of that. She was in a frisky mood after being

cooped up for so long. When no-one was looking she hid behind a tree. The Brownies walked on and didn't notice she was missing. When they were out of sight, Maisie left the path and went into the forest on her own. It was warm and the sun was streaming through the trees. Maisie was sure she could find her way back to the others, in a little while, once she had seen something interesting. She went further and further, skipping happily along and quite losing all sense of time.

By and by, the day wore on and Maisie began to feel hungry. She found a piece of tablet, a wee bit fluffy, in the pocket of her uniform, but that didn't fill her up. She decided that it was time to go back and she began to look for the path. She retraced her steps, but everything looked the same. She seemed to be going round in circles. At last it dawned on Maisie with a terrible shock that she was lost.

She was deep in the forest and it was growing dark. It no longer seemed friendly. There were strange cries and rustlings in the bushes and the wind wailed in the tops of the trees. Maisie ran this way and that, getting more and more anxious.

Then, far away among the trees, Maisie saw the glow of a fire. With a hopeful heart she made her way towards it. She could make out a group of shaggy, rough-looking cats gathered round the fire, dressed in torn plaids. One of them was playing a fiddle while others danced and sang and there was a delicious smell of cooking. Maisie's nose twitched, her mouth watered and she drew nearer.

The fiddler stopped playing and in the sudden silence, Maisie's tummy rumbled. Up jumped the leader of the band of cats. He peered into the darkness, waving a huge rusty sword and uttering a deep, bloodcurdling cry.

"Wha daur enter the camp o' Roderick McClartipaws? Up an' at them, lads! It's a raid!"

Then the whole gang of spitting, snarling, yowling, growling wild cats rose up and set off after Maisie. She took off as fast as her little paws would carry her, blundering through bog and heather. As she heard the skirling cries behind her draw nearer, Maisie grew desperate and searched about for somewhere to hide. At last she saw a dark entrance among some rocks and jumped inside.

She heard the savage mob thunder past and she breathed a sigh of relief. But she was still lost, hungry and worn out and her next sigh was a long and weary one.

"So much for Mrs McKitty's Highland hospitality," she muttered. "I wish I'd been a good little kitten," and a tear slipped down and trickled to the end of her whisker.

Suddenly she stiffened. She could hear something moving at the back of the cave. Maisie turned and peered into the gloom. There she saw a huge scaly creature with its breath pouring out of its nostrils like smoke. Terrified, Maisie began to tiptoe back towards the entrance of the cave. A loud roar stopped her in her tracks.

"Who's there?"

Maisie's courage deserted her.

"I'm only Maisie, a lost Brownie," she wailed. And then she burst into tears.

"Let me have a look at you," said the creature in a gentler voice. "Och, you're only a wee bit thing. I'm really sorry I gave you a fright."

Maisie wiped away her tears on her sleeve.

"I've never met a dragon before," she sniffed. "I thought you might want to eat me up. And," she added, "I've had a terrible day." She looked at him properly for the first time. He was smiling.

"Are you hungry?" he asked. "I never eat Brownies, myself, but I'm right fond of fish. I've got some fresh salmon here, on the fire. Why don't you join me and we'll have a wee blether."

The fish was delicious and soon filled Maisie's empty tum.

"Allow me to introduce myself," said her new friend. "I'm not a dragon, my name is Lachlan Mhor, better known as the Monster of Loch Ness."

"My word," said Maisie. "My Granny told me about you, but Mrs McKitty next door said you were just a lot of nonsense."

"Nonsense, is it?" snorted the Monster. "It's no joke being a Monster these days. I'm fed up with all the publicity. Do you know," he said, drawing closer to Maisie, "there's a wee submarine chugging up and down the Loch night and day, trying to take my photo? It's a right scunner."

He told her he used to go and watch shinty matches, but now the press were always after him. A sad look came into his eyes.

"It's lonely being a big star," he said.

"Do you not have any friends?" asked Maisie.

"Well," he said, more cheerfully, "once a year us Monsters get together at the Monster Mod. My cousins swim over from the Canadian Lakes and a crowd comes

from the Irish Loughs. We have a fine old ceilidh then."

Maisie laughed to think of it.

"But tell me about yourself," he said.

She told him about herself and how she'd got lost. And about the wild cats chasing her. The Monster scowled.

"So that Roderick McClartipaws is back, is he? Him and his gang would fight their own shadows, but they're scared of me. I'll soon drive them away. They won't stop running till they reach John o' Groats." Then he noticed that Maisie was beginning to yawn. "But first, I think I'd better be getting you back to your Brown Owl. She'll be worried about you."

Maisie climbed sleepily onto his back and Lachlan slid out of the cave, over the heather and into the Loch. He swam a short way and then set Maisie down on the bank.

"There's your hut over there," he said. "I'll leave you here, Maisie, and I want you to promise that you won't say a word to anyone about meeting me, or the newspapers will be after me and I'll have no peace at all, at all."

Maisie gave her word as a Brownie, and then kissed him goodbye.

"I'll away and terrorise the wild cats," he chuckled. "Goodbye, Maisie."

He slid back into the Loch and disappeared.

Maisie was just about to make her way to the hut when she heard someone calling her name. A crowd of Cubs, led by Archie and Hector carrying torches, rushed towards her.

"We've found you at last, Maisie," cried Archie, giving her a big hug.
Then the Cubs and their Akela led Maisie to the Brownie Hut. All the Brownies cheered at Maisie's return and began to ask her questions, but Brown Owl said that there would be plenty of time for questions tomorrow. She thanked the Cubs for bringing Maisie safely back and then put her to bed, where Maisie soon fell fast asleep.
Next day, Brown Owl told Maisie that she had been a very foolish kitten, but thanks

to the Cubs who were camping nearby all had ended well. Maisie was afraid that she might be drummed out of the Brownies, apologised for the worry she had caused and promised that she would always obey the Brownie Law in future.

And she was as good as her word. She even finished her knitting and got her badge.

On the last day of their holiday, the Brownies went into Inverness to buy presents for home. They bought postcards and sat on the grass outside the Castle where Maisie wrote one for her Daddy.

"Look Maisie," said Effie. "Your card's got a dragon on it."

Maisie shook her head.

"That's the Monster. He's too nice to be a dragon. He wouldn't hurt a fly."

"How do you know," asked a puzzled Effie.

"Just a feeling," said Maisie, smiling.

She finished her card.

"Dear Daddy," she had written, "I'm up North on my Brownie holiday. It was the rainy season up here, too, but it's better now. I got lost in the forest and met some wild cats, but the Cubs rescued me. Love, Maisie.

PS—I'm knitting you a scarf."

When it was time for lunch, Brown Owl gathered the Pack together and led them down to the riverbank, where they had their picnic. They all had such good appetites that there were few crumbs left over for the hungry sparrows that darted around their paws.

'This is lovely," sighed Effie. "It's like Blackford Pond."

"There are more ducks at Blackford Pond," said Maisie, munching the last of her sardine sandwich.

In the afternoon, they went to the Highland Games and saw big strong cats tossing the caber, throwing the hammer and putting the shot.

"Where are they putting it?" asked Effie, puzzled.

They listened to some stirring music from a pipe band and watched the Highland dancers competing on a raised platform. It was a great treat.

On that final evening, the Cubs came over and they had a barbecue and singsong together. The stars twinkled above the campfire and they ate sausages, baked potatoes and toasted marshmallows.

The Cubs entertained the Brownies, by singing some of their songs—although Archie and Hector never quite seemed to be in tune with each other, or anyone else—and then it was the Brownies' turn. After a few choruses, Maisie was called on for a solo and she merrily bawled out:

"Once a Brownie went to Camp, she went to Camp,
She went to Camp without a Lamp, without a Lamp,
And when she saw a Beetle in her Bed,
This is what the Brownie said, the Brownie said.
Beetle, Beetle, go away, go away,
I'm afraid you cannot stay, cannot stay,
For there is only one to a bed,
Only one to a Bed, to a Bed."

She received a great round of applause and munched happily on another sausage.

"Let's have a barbecue on the back green when we get home," said Hector.
"Oh yes," agreed Archie. "We can have the Morningside Highland Games."
"We can play at tossing the stretcher and throwing the welly," said Effie.
"And we can have a platform for Highland Dancing," suggested Flora.
"Maybe Mrs McKitty won't let us," wondered Archie, a little doubtfully.
"Oh, I don't know," grinned Maisie. "If we ask her to help organise it and be the judge . . . I can just imagine it!"

The flames of the campfire were just beginning to die, the Cubs and Brownies were quiet and sleepy.

"Morningside," murmured a drowsy Maisie. And she suddenly thought how nice it would be to see her dear Granny again. "There's no place like home," she purred.